The Proud Weed

WRITTEN BY SAMANTHA RAWLINGS

2021

The Proud Weed

Cataloging information
ISBN: 979-8-72886-061-7

Credits
Editor: Nicci Robinson @ Global Wordsmiths
Production Design: Nicci Robinson @ Global Wordsmiths

The Proud Weed

WRITTEN BY SAMANTHA RAWLINGS

2021

There once was a weed
who was 3 inches tall.
He grew from a gap
by a big red brick wall.

Each day he would ponder,
he just couldn't see,
what his purpose in life was,
that small yellow weed.

"I don't understand it,
I just cannot see,
why I'm here,
why I grow,
why I am,
why I'm me."

"For nobody likes a weed in their way.
They don't really know,
but I hear what they say.
They say I am ugly and shouldn't be here.
They don't look upon me
with love or with cheer."

Said a rose from a bush
that grew high up the fence,
"Don't worry, I'll tell you,
    I'll make you see sense."

"Please let me explain
    how important you are,
    to me and to others,
    from near and from far."

"You see, there's a reason
    that you are around,
    a reason you rise up and
    grow from the ground."

"You're very important.
You just cannot see,
that on top of your crown
sits a huge fluffy bee."

"This bee has awoken
from under the ground,
and now needs some help
from the flowers around."

"Your bright golden crown
is the first place they go.
They don't need a bouquet
or a big flower show."

"They need you to be there
So that they can survive.
And having you there
lets this bee really thrive."

The weed tried to look
to his crown for the bee.
He tried as he might,
but he just couldn't see

"So bees like my flower?" he sang out with glee.
"Oh yes," said the rose and the old apple tree.

The tree had been listening
from next to the shed
and joined in by saying...

"It should never be said
that weeds are not wanted
or of no use at all.

For it doesn't matter
how small or how tall,
a flowering plant is the best of them all."

The weed grew a smile
and stood proud by the wall.
And for once in his life,
he felt 5 inches tall.

"I just hadn't realised.
I just didn't know,
that magic can happen
from my little glow."

"My crown of bright yellow
is useful to some.
And my new way of thinking
has now just begun."

"My thanks to you, Rose
And to you, Apple Tree.
I'm much happier now,
and I'm proud to be me."

The sun set that day
in a beautiful way,
with colours of blue, red, and pink.
The weed settled down,
still proud of his crown,
and again, he started to think.

"If I help the bees
and so do the trees,
then work together, we must."

"When I'm ready to seed,
I'll ask the old tree
for a breeze…
No, no, for a gust."

"My seeds will be scattered
for mile after mile.
And soon they will grow
and help new bees to smile."

So, over the days
he started to seed.
And look at him now!
How handsome, indeed!

His crown of bright yellow
had changed over night
into something most splendid.
Oh, what a sight!

The weed was now ready
for new things to start.
He felt warm and fuzzy
in his little weed heart.

"Now I am ready,"
   the weed said with glee.

"Then I will start now,"
   said the old apple tree.

The tree started swaying
and caused a slight breeze.

But much more was needed
to set free these seeds.

Then the old tree swayed faster
and soon with a gust,
said, "This one should do it,
I'm sure that it must."

And right through the garden
the gust blew along.
And just for a second,
the weed had to hold on

The seeds started leaving,
1, 2, and 3,
with thanks to the wind
from that old apple tree.

They started their journeys,
and on they would go
to gardens, and fields,
and some pavements to grow.

Now the seeds had all gone,
and the weed had no crown.
But still he was happy,
not once did he frown.
He now knew his purpose.
He shouted out loud,
"I am a weed,
And I'll always be proud!"

Have you enjoyed The Proud Weed?

Let us know www.facebook.com/NatureProudSeries

And watch out for the next adventure

in the Nature Proud series:

The Lonely Worm

Editing & production
Global Wordsmiths
& Global Words Press

What's Your Story?

www.globalwords.co.uk

Printed in Great Britain
by Amazon